And The Walls Came
Tumbling Down

William S. Moody

authorHOUSE®

AuthorHouse™
1663 Liberty Drive
Bloomington, IN 47403
www.authorhouse.com
Phone: 1 (800) 839-8640

Published by AuthorHouse 10/18/2017

ISBN: 978-1-5462-0731-3 (sc)
ISBN: 978-1-5462-0730-6 (e)

"They must turn from evil and do good; they must seek peace and pursue it." 1 Peter 3:11

This work of fiction examines the possibility of sophisticated Western European countries being legally overthrown by Islamic groups using the ballot box as the vehicle to achieve their goal. A well-organized migration of Islamic faithful to the United Kingdom ensures that with time, Western Europe becomes part of the Caliphate which ultimately will control Saudi Arabia, Syria, Iran and Iraq.

The United States gets drawn into the changing world order and apart from giving sanctuary to United Kingdom interests, suddenly finds itself coping with change, the pressure for which comes from the states themselves.

Russia and China begin to emerge as major players and as Russia rebuilds its empire, it takes advantage of the fiscal disarray in the United States and offers a substantial sum of money to purchase Alaska. A deal is done: Alaska rejoins the Russian Empire.

However, other states have been carefully watching the Alaska deal and now look at their own options.

Dedication

To my wife, Marian, without whose encouragement
and help, this book would still be a dream.

Foreword

There are those who will be glad to read that this may be my one and only book

whilst others will consider it - as the English say as

"A cracking good yarn sprinkled with some facts, but mainly fantasy".

A well-known phrase comes to mind which aptly describes the core of the book:

Evil prospers when good men stand by and do nothing.

Nothing new or earth-shattering in that statement, so here goes...

Chapter 1

An Inglorious Plot

Underground meeting places were numerous within the labyrinths of the City of Tehran and had been prepared some years ago to prevent electronic surveillance by the United States and its allies.

On a Spring day during 2010, the unthinkable was happening. A meeting was reaching its conclusion between the two most powerful men in the Islamic world - the leader of the Sunni Muslims and his counterpart for the Shiite Muslims.

Men with different ideologies but united in one desire, the domination of the world by Islam.

The older cleric leaned back in his chair, studied his notes and spoke. "Well, here it is then. We are agreed that we cannot defeat the great Satan by military means alone. Their advanced technology and their arming of Israel and Saudi Arabia make it impossible to secure an Islamic Caliphate in the Middle East within the foreseeable future. We must look elsewhere to secure our victory and perhaps we could refine Ghandi's approach of non-violent opposition. However,

Ghandi secured his success by removing the British from India whereas our objective is on a far greater scale and will take many years to come to fruition.

We are agreed that the answer lies in Western Europe and in our ability to manipulate the political system of each country to elect Muslims to city and local councils, and then have Muslims to stand for election to the national bodies that actually govern those countries.

It will be necessary to boost migration of our brothers to Europe and to encourage Muslim parents to raise much larger families so that within a period of years, maybe as few as 50, we will have built up a major presence in each country able to influence the voting pattern and then obtain a voting majority in as many parliaments as possible.

With such a majority and over a period of time, we will be able to usher in a new Muslim majority in nearly every Western European country. Our dreams of a Muslim Caliphate stretching from Saudi Arabia to the Atlantic coast will be realized and will be the base for expansion to other continents.

We have agreed to instruct all our Imams to communicate our decision to the faithful and the immigration program and enlargement of the family units should begin immediately.

Our primary target country will be the United Kingdom".

Chapter 2

A Prime Ministerial Broadcast

The 2015 election in the United Kingdom had resulted in the return of a dominant Conservative government and Prime Minister Justin Marshall had lost no time in telling his television audience that it had been a great victory. He spent little time however, in telling the electorate that his majority was only possible with support from minor political parties in Northern Ireland, some reliance on a "breakaway" group called

"The United Kingdom Independent Party" and a little noted but growing caucus of Muslims within the Conservative party.

Equally un-noticed was a small number of Muslims in the opposition Labour party ranks. A combination of the two groups meant that they would have some 30 of the 650 seats available in the British House of Commons.

The Imams were quietly and methodically doing their job.

Chapter 3

A Gentle Progress

The years passed and the Imams worked with their people encouraging greater participation in political affairs. Islamists were standing for election to city and local councils and with the growing Muslim population, were comfortably winning their seats.

The United Kingdom population of Muslims in 2015 was two million; in the local elections of 2030 it had grown to five million and by 2040, with national elections in 2042 it was almost ten million. Every major northern and southern city was now controlled by Muslims and the national election returned a total of 120 Muslims to the British parliament. A government where the majority of members were Muslim was probable within ten to fifteen years. It was noticed that emigration to Canada, Australia, New Zealand and other Non-Muslims countries was running at a level never before seen. Non-Muslims were clearly aware of the trend that there was a net exodus of people falling from the United Kingdom population.

Chapter 4

Recognition at Last

The new United Kingdom Prime Minister, Anthony Brown, sat in the cabinet room with his deputy William Peters, and the foreign secretary Rupert Andrews. It was early June 2042 and the new government, led by Brown had been in power one month.

The Prime Minister spoke first. "This report from the electoral office confirms what we have known for some time." He put the documents down and continued. "Within a short period of time, the Islamists in both parties will collectively have a national majority and will be able to rule this country as they see fit. What are our options?"

Bill Peters shook his head. "We are a democracy and unless we are going to consider declaring permanent States of Emergency or limiting immigration numbers or even introducing a policy of repatriating Muslims back to Africa and the Middle East we have no choice but to let the situation take its course."

"You do realize what you're saying?" said Rupert Andrews. "Once they gain power they will remove the King and all the

Royal Family; the Church of England will be banished as will all forms of religion except Islam. All our institutions such as the Stock Exchange and the press will cease to exist." He paused for a moment.

"What about our military falling under their control? What about the freedom and privacy of Non-Muslim nationals, who is going to speak for them. Will they be required to become Muslim?"

After a brief silence Rupert Andrews spoke again. "I have only instanced a few of the myriad of problems we would need to address. In short, I believe we are faced with a return to the dark ages."

An all embracing silence settled on the Cabinet Room as each politician considered the magnitude of the problem now before them. After what seemed an eternity, the Prime Minister spoke. "I need to meet with the President of the United States and if possible with the leaders of Australia, Canada, New Zealand and South Africa, India and Pakistan."

Chapter 5

The Master Plan

Coincidentally, at about that time, the two current Islamic leaders were concluding their meeting.

The younger of the two summed up the situation.

"It is almost 30 years since the first meeting was held and each year the Islamic cause has advanced exponentially. Thanks to Isis and other similar groups Saudi Arabia and Syria have fallen; the UK government will collapse, with France and Germany following within another 10 years. The rest of Europe including Turkey and the Low Countries will be absorbed quickly."

The older cleric added, "The UK will be the first European country to be assimilated into the Caliphate.

We must start planning now and we must bring together our brightest minds. Let us start with the appointment of committees to take over the running of the country and also to recommend which institutions will continue for the time being. I am thinking for example of the Bank of England and the manner in which we replace the pound sterling with our own currency. The euro currency will just fall away. We must also consider the impact on international commerce particularly with the British Commonwealth countries and what response we can expect from the Americans.

Everything we have done to achieve our position has been legal and non-violent and given the state of the American economy I cannot imagine any military response coming from them."

The two were silent and thoughtful for a moment.

The older cleric gathered his thoughts and continued. "Perhaps the greatest problem is how we deal with the major religious groups, not only in the United Kingdom which is prominently Church of England, and the rest of Europe which is mainly Roman Catholic.

Our more radical brothers will wish to see these institutions eliminated immediately."

He sat back and thought more deeply about what he had just said and continued, "I would be in favor of a long period of integration but with our religious teachings beginning in schools and in all education facilities immediately. Let one of the committees begin work on this issue now. All senior church personnel from any denomination should be encouraged to relocate to other spheres of religious activity. I note for example, major expansion of activity within the Catholic Church aimed at building up their presence in South America and South Africa."

The clerics did not address the military issues. The thinking was that naval, air and army units would be integrated into a "Caliphate" military force. Since the fall of Saudi Arabia, an enormous supply of American made armaments had been acquired and the Caliphates military force would be substantially larger with the addition of units provided by the fall of the United Kingdom and other countries.

It had to be assumed that America, with its sophisticated weaponry would continue to protect Israel but how long this status could be contained was a matter of long term conjecture.

Most certainly however, America would be obliged to consider its position regarding weapons of mass destruction operated mainly in Scotland.

Chapter 6

A Visit to the United States

The British Prime Minister, Anthony Brown, was met at Dulles airport and whisked off to the British Embassy to prepare for tomorrow's meeting with the President. The following day he would meet heads of governments from various British Commonwealth countries.

Brown was acutely aware that he was coming to Washington at a time when America had very serious problems of its own. The national debt level was out of control; a situation existed in the House and Senate that could best be described as stagnant; continued high levels of public unrest over civil rights issues and a persistently high crime rate, the like of which was unprecedented.

Coupled with the failure to introduce effective gun control the American public were in a very nervous state about the direction that their country was taking.

To make matters worse, prior administrations had cut back on America's military, both at home and abroad. This had made it easy for China, and to a lesser extent, Russia, to fill the void left behind by the Americans such that their prestige as a world leader had been seriously impaired.

This was not the best time for the British Prime Minister to be coming to Washington to add to the President's problems.

Chapter 7

An Imperfect Solution

As far as the American President was concerned, the old adage that 'you can please some of the people all of the time and all of the people some of the time' was nonsense. He had been in office for three years and could categorically say that you can't please all of the people any of the time whether they're democrat or republican.

The 72 year old Republican from Texas was visibly showing the strains of his office and many times had privately wondered if the current political system could survive in its present form. Today, however, was being spent with his long time friend, the British Prime Minister. There would be meetings in the morning followed by lunch and then an afternoon of golf and a formal White House reception in the evening.

The introduction formalities complete and official photographs taken, the group sat down for coffee. The only other person there by request of the Prime Minister was Tom Sanchez, the American Secretary of State.

The Prime Minister spoke for an hour without interruption.

When he had finished, the President stood and walked over to the large window in the Oval Office and quietly contemplated the disaster facing the United Kingdom. Eventually he turned to the Prime Minister. "When do you anticipate they will gain control?' "Possibly by the next national elections in 2062, definitely by the 2072 election," replied the Prime Minister. The President turned to his Secretary of State and asked.

"Tom, what are our options?" The ex-lawyer thought deeply then replied. "Quite frankly, there are few options. First, the Royal Family must be removed either to the US or to one or more Commonwealth countries. Then, there must be a 'British government in exile' in a chosen location which I believe should be near to the American center of government. Furthermore, we must address the status of the United Kingdom's military assets. They must not fall into unfriendly hands. All naval and air force units must be relocated and any advanced technology such as is located at Cheltenham must also be removed. All necessary personnel and families must relocate - this can be done under the cover of military exercises.

Steps must be taken to protect and extract religious leaders, and somehow we must encourage people of Jewish origin to emigrate. Israel is the obvious place although we can expect other countries including us to open our doors wider. All UK overseas embassies and personnel must come under the control of the British government in exile. There will undoubtedly be pivotal politicians and civil servants to cater for.

What will be the position of the Bank of England and the pound sterling? I imagine that both will cease to exist. Plans must be drawn up to remove all gold and other specie to a new location."

The secretary paused for a moment. "We probably have five years at the most so that takes us to 2062. It would be foolish to assume that the UK government would last beyond that date but if it does it will be a bonus in helping us with our planning. It will not be long before the population starts to figure out what is going on so my bet is we have five years to plan and to have in place the action that must be taken.

In short, we must move now and create the necessary joint committees and put them to work. Prime Minister, you must brief your Commonwealth representative to obtain their reaction and an indication as to what help they are able to give." The President and the Prime Minister were in a state of shock as they contemplated the enormity of the task before them.

Chapter 8

Advise and Assist

The President left to convene a meeting with his Vice President as well as the Speaker of the House and the Democratic and Republican party leaders. He wanted to alert them early to the problem and to be in agreement with whatever actions that he could legally take without having to go through the House and Senate. He firmly believed he would get full support on this issue because so many of the American people had their roots in countries that were facing the same fate. Italy, France and Germany to name but a few. For his part, the Prime Minister had already set up an afternoon meeting with Commonwealth leaders from Australia, New Zealand, Canada, South Africa, India and Pakistan.

Again, the US Secretary of State was present and he and the Prime Minister essentially gave the leaders the same presentation as had been given to the President. Suffice to say that none of the leaders were surprised, and all were anxious to be of help in providing facilities for military assets and personnel. The prospect of the 'Royals' moving to their country seemed to outweigh any other issues. The meeting concluded with all parties promising to write to the Prime Minister confirming what help they could offer both militarily and domestically.

The Prime Minister returned to the UK the following day. He would convene meetings with key people from business, military, religious, and political worlds and agree with them a timetable for the break up of a way of life that had been brought about by a peaceful but sinister faction.

Chapter 9

The Russians are Coming

As early as 2010 the Russians had started a program for the re-acquisition of areas of their old empire that for various reasons had been lost to them - as they saw it. There had been military action to take back part of Georgia, an incursion into the Ukraine under the guise of a "separatist" operation, and there had been the integration of the Crimea. The "Russian Bear' was making itself known and was threatening other territories which it felt should rejoin what is now the Russian Federation. Verbal threats to some of the "Stans" were commonplace.

All this, while America and its allies failed to stand up to the Russian aggression in Europe and merely introduced financial sanctions which would hurt in the short term only. For many years the world watched as Russia grew stronger. Successive American administrations did nothing and this leaderless situation only led to the 'Bear' becoming stronger and more aggressive and eventually more ambitious in its demands. With perfect timing, their most audacious demand came out of the blue. In a letter from the Russian President a proposal was made that Alaska should be returned to Russian ownership and a sum of six trillion dollars would be paid to the United States of America.

As part of the transaction, Alaska would become an independent economic unit within the Russian Federation and the population of Alaska would continue to enjoy its existing rights such as property ownership; protection of assets; job security and the right to emigrate to the contiguous United States any time. These rights would be guaranteed for a period of 100 years.

The American President presented the proposal to his cabinet and they all spent the next half hour laughing and joking about selling off an American state, until, that is, the Secretary of the Treasury asked for quiet in order to speak."As amusing as this may seem," he began, "nearly all the land mass of Alaska is owned by the Federal Government and there would be no reason why the government could not sell all or part of Alaska. In the foreseeable future, dependence on oil will be reducing and any alternative to identify and extract other minerals would be expensive. It could be a good time to dispose of what may be considered as an underperforming asset.

Finally, our national debt stands at thirty trillion dollars. My guess is that we can negotiate them up to say, ten trillion which could be applied to reduce our national debt and the interest charges associated with it. The land mass of Alaska is 600,000 square miles with a population density of one person per square mile. In the scale of things, apart from some loss of prestige for the United States, I would say that we should give serious consideration to this proposal."

Chapter 10

Closing the Deal

A subdued cabinet then discussed the pros and cons of the Russian offer and eventually voted to form an exploratory committee to consider in greater detail the feasibility of the proposal. Eventually, after hundreds of hours of meetings, a way forward was approved to open formal negotiations with the Russian Federation. These negotiations took three years to complete such that by 2070 Alaska formally became part of the Russian Federation.

There was little fanfare or celebration. A disillusioned American public welcomed good news wherever it could be found and the final price received by the Federal government for the sale was eight and a half trillion dollars having held back one and a half trillion dollars which had been reserved for Alaskan families to provide incentives for them to stay. In the United States, with the sale of Alaska, the first part of the wall had tumbled.

Chapter 11

The Ayes Have It

With the result of the 2062 general election now known, the political wall in the United Kingdom started to tumble and within five years the political walls surrounding the rest of Europe, parts of Asia and Africa and the entire Middle East would also fall. The Muslim caucus was now in control of the UK. The House of Commons and the House of Lords were abolished and replaced with regional committees whose membership was exclusively Muslim. Sharia law replaced the British legal systems and the practicing of all forms of religion other than Islam was forbidden. The education system was replaced and females were relegated to a subservient status. Those people of Jewish origin had been given a small amount of time to relocate. Fortunately, much rumor had preceded the election result and most people of Jewish persuasion had already fled the country. A British government in exile had been formed in Washington DC. and an act of congress was necessary for the British government to purchase land and buildings. Other representative UK offices in the United

States and its world-wide embassies would now report to the Washington DC office.

Military equipment and personnel had been dispersed to new bases in countries around the world and the British nuclear submarine fleet was temporarily based in Norfolk, Virginia. Air Force units were relocated to Canada. Hundreds of other changes were made in the years leading up to 2062 but to most of the UK and countless others around the world the safe relocation of the Royal Family was of major importance. The King was the symbol of continuity and would continue to enjoy the loyalty of his people in the UK and elsewhere. Canada had provided homes and other facilities for the King and his family while other royal members had taken up residences in Australia, New Zealand and South Africa. In a few brief years the political, economic and religious map of the world had changed. It would take much time for people to adjust to the new regime, and there was little doubt that Islam would continue to flourish in its pursuit of world domination.

In America however, where capitalism was still alive and well, covetous eyes had been watching and waiting for a suitable opportunity to arise which would have far greater consequences for the world's most powerful country. That opportunity started to manifest itself in the spring of 2060.

Chapter 12

A Changing of the Guard

The Mexican-American war of 1848 had resulted in an American victory which in turn had led to the transfer of some fifty per cent of the land mass of Mexico to the United States. That land mass was principally made up of California, Texas, Arizona, New Mexico and Nevada. In the space of 200 years most of these states had become economic powerhouses with California alone being the world's sixth largest economy.

Along with the expansion of industry and commerce came the need for a growing workforce and although many skilled and well educated people came to the old Mexican states the greatest number were people of Hispanic background. They provided the cheap labor to fuel the economic miracles of California and Texas. As time passed there came an awareness that a considerable number were illegal immigrants who quite simply just walked across the Mexican border and set up home mainly in California.

Successive United States administrations had ignored the issue until back in 2005 when a census established that the population of California was some 36 million people and that in addition there were at least another 10 million illegal residents. By 2015, the Hispanic population both legal and illegal was the largest minority group in California, and by 2060 would be in the majority at 45 million out of a total population of 60 million. California would in essence become a Mexican state and change would become inevitable.

Chapter 13

Change Down Mexico Way

The Mexican president, Alberto Sanchez laid down his copy of the latest census for California. It showed that indeed, the Californian population would hit 60 million by 2060 and that Hispanics will make up seventy five per cent of the population. The President spoke to his cabinet who were gathered around a large boardroom table.

"You will note that the twenty five per cent minority are mainly white, are well educated and well paid but more and more of them are leaving California to live and work in Texas, Arizona and the increasingly popular state of Nevada which is now a major hi-tech destination. The principal reasons for this migration is high personal taxation and the mass of rules and regulations that literally swamp individuals, commerce and industry. It must be obvious that unless something is done, a quarter of the population which includes the leaders, entrepreneurs, educators, in other words the prime movers, will just trickle away and California will become an agricultural-based economy and unable to support its population base which will be almost exclusively Hispanic". The ministers each spoke for a few minutes and there seemed be a consensus that preferential loans should be offered to companies willing to stay in California and also to attract companies who had moved out of state provided they relocate back to California. There was some general conversation between them all and then the room became quiet when everyone turned to listen to President Alberto Sanchez.

"I have a far more radical proposal for you to consider that if approved will enable California to return to its status as a province of Mexico. It's a question of timing", the Mexican President continued. "America is on the edge of a financial abyss. There is talk of a collapse of the monetary system, and inward investment into the United States has slowed to a trickle. Confidence levels in the United States have been seriously eroded, and their international debt which was substantially reduced with the sale of Alaska, has now returned to unmanageable proportions". The president paused. "Since the days of the Obama administration it has been the policy of successive democratic presidents to encourage the transfer of wealth from one section of society to another, from the top ten per cent of earners and wealth creators to the middle and working classes. This continues to this day and these persistent tax impositions show no sign of any reversal of policy. Consequently, money has flowed from the wealth earners to the wealth spenders and the net result is that there is no motivation for the 'movers and shakers' to invest in or remain in the United States. It seems to me that the first step is a one-on-one meeting with the governor of California, Gilberto Torres, and then a referendum to ascertain the views of California residents. It should be kept simple and they should be asked if they prefer California to continue to be part of the United States or to cede from the union and revert to being a province of Mexico. I would suggest that we would need a majority of three quarters of those voting in favor in order for us to commence negotiations with the United States"

The meeting was adjourned and President Sanchez asked that each minister take time to consider the concept and to meet for further discussion in three weeks.

Chapter 14

Lone Star on the Horizon

President Sanchez had been a long time friend and admirer of the fiery Texas Governor Paul J. Peters III. The lone star state had always had a reputation for being more independent than other states. Federalism was a dirty word and many influential Texans, the governor included, felt that Texas, and maybe a few other states, would be better off on their own. The Texas Governor had called for a meeting the previous week and apart from he and the Mexican President, the only other person present was the Governor of California - the Hispanic Governor of California, Gilberto Torres.

Peters began. "We have all spoken on the telephone about our concerns for the future of not only the United States but by extension the future of the peoples and sovereign states that we represent. The Federal Government's borrowings from the international capital markets have now reached the point where even the repayment of the interest charges may not to be met. Social unrest has been created by a population of people living primarily on entitlements. Penal federal and state income tax has ensured that large numbers of entrepreneurs have left the state and the federal government's interference in the capitalist system has led to job losses running at a level that cannot be sustained. Social unrest over civil rights issues continue to plague each state and we are slowly but surely moving towards a state of anarchy. I want none of this for Texas, but how do you feel?"President Sanchez looked thoughtfully at the other two. The Governor of California was the first to respond. "What we are thinking of may very well contribute to encouraging a state of anarchy within the United States and some may accuse us of committing treason. My own government is acutely aware of the insurmountable problems faced by the Federal government and to the extent that they may adversely affect the Hispanic people, then my government would support whatever action is necessary to ensure a better way of life for so many people. My government would be primarily concerned with the State of California and provided we abide by the rule of the ballot box and the requirements of any constitutional committees, then I think we should commence proceedings, either collectively or independently with the Federal government for California to be returned to Mexico. It's been obvious for many years that the State of California has been in terminal decline" He paused to gather his thoughts and then continued. "Successive federal administrations did nothing to solve the problem of the illegal immigrants entering our states; their children come from traditionally large families and as the generations have passed, we have seen our population increase to nearly 60 million. At the same time the state administration, controlled by the Democratic party has made life so much easier by continually granting larger entitlements to an ever increasing unemployment pool. The politicians in turn look to private industry to pick up the additional costs financed by tax increases. As a consequence, employers have left our state and relocated to more welcoming states like Nevada. I will back any action that will lead to a resurgence of California's fortunes. The Governor of Texas interjected, "Texas has not suffered to the same extent as other states. Employment levels are good, we encourage companies to relocate to us, and we offer attractive commercial loans and preferential tax concessions to both existing and start-up businesses. We have seen our state prosper, the population is approaching 40 million and the outlook is good were it not for a federal government that is out of control. The cost of federalism is like a yoke around our neck. I know that governors of other states feel that the time is right to go to the voters in each of our states and ask them if they wish to remain in the United States as currently constituted, or if they wish to become an independent country." The wall continued to crumble but at a faster pace.

Chapter 15

The Genie is out of the Bottle

On September 1st. 2055, California gave notice to the Federal government that it would hold a referendum which would simply ask its citizens if they wished to continue as part of the United States of America or revert back to being a sovereign state of Mexico. The totally predictable result was in favor of a return to Mexico and although there would now be endless meetings of constitutional committees; countless legal challenges in the courts and a myriad of decisions to make, the ball had gathered momentum. Perhaps the greatest challenge was the need to get the House and Senate to vote in favor of allowing California to go. Pressure would come from surprising sources. Texas's plan to cede from the Union had now expanded to include Arizona, New Mexico and Nevada. Meetings had been held between the governors and as with California they would ask their citizens to approve a deal but this time it was to be part of an independent country styled as 'The New South Western States of America'.

The proposal was put to voters on March 1st, 2057 and was overwhelmingly approved. The inevitable screams of

'Outrageous' and 'Treasonous' were frequently heard from the House and Senate but those members with a little more foresight could see the writing on the wall. The fact that Texas's bid for independence had been presented at the same time as negotiations for releasing California was no coincidence and suddenly there came the realization that other states might see an opportunity for independence and also for revenge.

Chapter 16

When Johnny Comes Marching Home Again

There was of course an undercurrent of mistrust and dislike that had existed between the southern states and the northern states since the end of the civil war. Rumors about Texas, itself an old rebel state had been circulating for months; the result was a meeting of the governors of Florida, Georgia, North Carolina, South Carolina, Virginia, Maryland and Delaware. The proposal for independence was passed and a newly formed country would be established called the Southern States of America. There was now nothing stopping the momentum. The deal was presented to the House and the Senate three weeks before the vote to release California.

The pressure was too great and the House and Senate voted in favor. Everyone knew that it was only a matter of time before the United States of America ceased to exist.

Chapter 17

The Final Curtain Call

Washington State, Oregon, Colorado, Idaho, Montana. Wyoming and Utah became part of the 'North West States of America'. Kansas, North and South Dakota, Nebraska and Oklahoma became part of the 'Central States of America'.

Minnesota, Iowa, Wisconsin, Illinois, Michigan, Indiana, Ohio together with Hawaii formed the 'Independent States of America'.

New York, Pennsylvania, Massachusetts, New Jersey, Vermont, New Hampshire, Connecticut, Rhode Island, Delaware and Maine formed the 'Northern States of America'.

Finally Missouri, Arkansas, Mississippi, Alabama, Tennessee, Louisiana, Virginia, West Virginia, North and South Carolina, Kentucky, Florida and Georgia decided to call themselves the 'Confederate States of America'. They would collectively be referred to as 'The Five States' but each was in effect, an independent country.

Washington DC would continue to be an administrative center for common services that all the Five States would need. The future of the American Territories such as Puerto

Rico and American Samoa was yet to be decided. With five new nations being created there was much to be done and a target date of October 1st. 2060 was agreed. The congress would be dissolved, new parliaments created in each capital city, elections, abolishment of the Supreme Court, setting up of new judiciary, national stock exchanges created, police, security and fire controls and all this was just the tip of the iceberg. It was decided to keep military assets under one agency, the cost of which would be borne by each separate country or state allocated on a 'population' basis. The same was agreed regarding the CIA, the FBI and other national security agencies which would continue as separate organizations. It would of course take many years for all the work to be done that will result in five new major countries.

In the early 1990s the Economic and Monetary Unit of the European Union tried to bring about political, monetary and trading cohesion to some 30 countries and after some 60 years or so is still working on trying to achieve their objective. Back in the 1970s, President Nixon asked Mao-Tse Tung what he thought were the consequences of the French Revolution. "Too early to tell," replied Mao. Perhaps the same question will be asked of the five new countries in say, one hundred years from now.

Chapter 18

In Memoriam

Four events contributed to the downfall of the United States and they were all to do with the Middle East. The first was the famous 'drawing the red line in the sand' statement designed to stop then President Assad of Syria and protect refugees from that country being slaughtered in their thousands. Predictably, nothing was done and the United States' stellar reputation took a major hit to its worldwide prestige. Next, the withdrawal of the majority of the United States combat troops and those of its allies, against Pentagon advice, left a massive vacuum in the Middle East which was quickly filled by rival Islamist fighters. The third event to contribute to the downfall was that eventually the United States sent back small numbers of advisory personnel but it was too late and the US suffered another black eye. Finally, the Tehran agreement was universally condemned by everyone other than those who negotiated it. Among other things, to turn over one hundred and fifty billion dollars to the world's largest sponsor of state terrorism seemed to the average American to be crass stupidity. When it was later discovered that two rival groups of Islamic fighters were at the same time both being financed by the United States, an un-nerved American public rushed to grab whatever was available to return their lives to some semblance of order.

A new start with one of the new countries being created seemed something worthy of support and a path to a better future, regardless of the menacing presence from the Islamic Caliphate in Europe.

Chapter 19

The Way Forward

The affairs of churches everywhere tend to crawl along at a snail's pace and are steeped in centuries of time rather than the three score years and ten that are arbitrarily allotted to we mortals at birth. To take an example; 1,100 years or so ago the Russian Eastern Church split from the Roman Catholic Church and little was done to repair the rupture. Some 500 years ago Henry the Eighth created the Church of England by splitting from the Roman Church and nothing was done to repair that breach, which is all the more remarkable because the meeting just beginning had been called by his Holiness the Pope, Clement XV three weeks before and present in that room were three churchmen who may well be involved in dictating the course of world events over the next few years. Two clerics were present in body and mind: Bishop Alan Smith representing the Church of England together with the Patriarch of the Russian Orthodox Church, Mikhail Davydenka. The third churchman joining the meeting by satellite was Pope Clement. The main meeting was being held in an office complex just outside Brasilia to where much of the Roman Catholic administration had relocated well before the collapse of Western Europe. The Pope was calling from Rio de Janeiro which was now the main spiritual center for Catholics throughout the world. The meeting was being recorded; the date was January 31, 2100. His Holiness began the proceedings with a brief prayer and then addressed his two listeners. "Information has reached us of a massive expansion plan being prepared by Islamic terrorists which if allowed to succeed will put them well on the way to world domination, which you will recall has always been their objective. This plan must not be allowed to progress." The Pope then outlined what he knew.

"The Islamic terror groups wish to contain and ultimately control Russia and China and they would do this by blocking the international trading routes of both countries. Over a period of several years, the Islamists would also invade the "rice bowl" countries and then move on to Indonesia and the Philippines. Taiwan, North and South Korea and Japan would finally fall and any remaining territories in the East and South China Seas would be quickly absorbed. They would then be able to exercise incredible influence over Russia and China. We must not forget that Western Europe and the Middle East, both Islamic strongholds can also block those routes to Russia. Literally billions of tons of cargo flow over these routes and if their plan is allowed to proceed then within a relatively short time our churches will no longer exist in Asia and what remains of Europe. What gentlemen, are your suggestions?"The Russian patriarch spoke first. "I assume the Islamists have the military equipment and knowledge to conduct such a military adventure. I further assume that India and Bangladesh will stay out of this and that Pakistan, being an Islamic republic will sit on the fence".

The Pope nodded his head in agreement. "So much equipment was acquired and modernized and Jordan and Saudi Arabia have always been centers of excellence for military training. The terrorists are more than capable of putting together a formidable fighting force." "Then," said the Russian, "and God forgive me for saying so, but we must meet with our political masters to discuss options available should this control of the trade routes and any potential invasions take place."

Chapter 20

The Americans to the Rescue

The Church of England bishop, Alan Smith, could not add much to the Russian Patriarch's response. He realized that if a military option developed, this could involve other parts of the world particularly Africa where Islamists had already infiltrated many countries on that continent. South America, he thought, being eighty per cent Catholic would be fine. However, he made one vital point. "We must keep the five North American States in the loop. All five are now constituted under a National Council, and we would be dealing with one person authorized to speak for all of the council. I am sure they are already aware of the looming danger that will have consequences for them. Also, cutting off trade with Taiwan and Japan would cause an enormous upheaval in maritime trade, and I suspect that Japan and the Five States will suffer the most. Over the many years since the breakup of the old United States, the new American States have contained the Islamic terror threat but this proposed manipulation of goods going to and from Russia and China would have serious implications for them. I say again, the Five American States through their council must be involved immediately.

Within two weeks a dossier was prepared which, although only a summary of the position to date, also set out various options that the Islamists might adopt should they proceed with their plan. The circulation list was pretty impressive and included the Pope, the Russian and Chinese presidents, the British and Australian prime ministers and the National Council President representing the five North American States. Strangely, no initial response had yet been received from the National Council member for the Five States but all agreed to meet in Beijing, China on February 15th. 2100.

There really was no way of avoiding the issue. The problem was Russia and China and by a long drawn-out process each country could be slowly strangled to death by introducing blockades backed up by strong naval support. The Islamist navy consisted of vessels acquired from western navies and funded by billions of dollars paid from oil reserves to purchase new warships, built ironically in China and Russia. The Islamist navy had, amongst its arsenal, aircraft carriers, state of the art cruisers and numerous vessels that would function as landing craft. Thus they would have the ability to occupy the "rice bowls" before moving on to Japan. "This really is a dilemma." said the Chinese president. "Any meaningful military response by any of us would involve nuclear strikes which in turn would kill millions in the hugely populated countries of India, Pakistan and Bangladesh. China itself would suffer badly from nuclear contamination and may be unable to feed some or all of its enormous population." "What happens to China will happen to Russia," said the Russian President. He paused for a moment. "By the way, is the Council President of the Five States coming to this meeting today?"As if on cue, the security doors to the room opened and it was announced that Mr. Harold Metz, representing the Five States was joining the meeting. "Gentlemen," he commenced, "I have a statement to make and I will need to take your response with me when I leave later tonight.

Chapter 21

A Solution at Hand

"The problem is that over a long period and, by the way, the terrorist groups are good at being patient, it is our view that slowly narrowing or closing trade routes will eventually be successful." The Council President paused and waited for his comments to sink in. He continued, "They have the money, the manpower and other resources to wage a long and cruel campaign which raises the awful specter of great numbers of our young military, who are the lifeblood of our nations, being lost on countless battlefields." The Chinese President and the Russian President remained respectfully silent wondering where this was all going. The Council President continued. "For a few years when the Five States first became independent they acted as such and there was little cooperation between them that could be described as being for the general good. "Clearly the National Council only deals with matters which may adversely affect the Five States or, threaten their collective wellbeing. After a few years it was obvious that terrorism on our mainland was our biggest exposure and we felt sure that the Islamists at some point would wish to bring North America under their sphere of influence."

The Council President continued. "We could see therefore that in a relatively short time we would be involved in hostilities of some kind. After the breakup of the old United States the military was run down to be a purely maintenance function. This made the Five States vulnerable to attack and caused us to take a long term review of our military needs. It is important that I now have your undivided attention because we believe that we can ultimately defeat and eliminate the world wide threat posed by Islam."

Given that the others present in the room could so far neither offer or make any pertinent suggestions, the Council President, who seemed to grow in stature with every passing minute continued. "Fifteen years ago we decided to pursue the concept of developing smart weapons that relied not on bullets, bombs or missiles but rather by a new source of energy. If it could be created it would not kill or wound but rather control and contain enemy combatants and be able to operate over vast areas. A very wonderful 'space age' concept but as yet only on the drawing board. However, years of research has produced a control system that jumped two generations in efficiency. I will at this stage tell you only what it is capable of. For now the technology must remain with the Five States."A few questions were asked but everyone wanted to move on and listen to the Council President's plan."In our view we are facing reconstruction and renewal on a massive scale and we must start the relocation of the Arab peoples back to their countries of origin." He paused and then continued on."Voluntary if possible, forcibly if needs be but with no harm or injury to those being removed. We will enlist the help of moderate Islamists who after having witnessed demonstrations of our new technology will be only too happy to work with all of us to return to normalcy and rid the world of the evil of this Islamic caliphate. Unless we stop them, in the next five years they may well achieve the world domination they seek."

The Chinese President raised his hand. "Get to the point. What can this technology do and is it to be supported by military action?" "No," said the Council President most emphatically, "Absolutely not."

After a welcome coffee break, it was explained that scientists from the Five States had worked on a new energy source combining certain parts of a lithium battery with super energy and conductivity from cold fusion energy. This is not the lithium used to create batteries for cars but is a thousand-fold more powerful. Cold fusion has been described as 'energy that drives the stars' and only recently were our scientists able to combine and produce a source of energy that is greater than anything on earth.

More silence followed and some of the people were now beginning to see the path ahead. The Council President further explained. "The machine will throw out a beam or several beams if necessary which will be invisible to the naked eye. The beam will create a grid system and when it is charged or ionized it will disable every piece of military equipment within its boundaries. Those boundaries can extend many miles from the control center, and for example, a group of six control centers could operate an area the size of Western Europe."

Now the enormity of the achievement hit everyone in the room. It was the Russian President who rose to his feet. "But what about the Islamic terrorists and their sympathizers; there are now many millions of them and how do you deal with the reconstruction and renewal you spoke of earlier." "Well now," said the Council President. "This is the most amazing thing. When the grid system is in force, all forms of life will continue within the grid but nothing or no-one may leave or cross its boundaries. It all revolves around devising a system whereby Islamic terrorists are taken from the grids where they have been held but not restrained and repatriated to their countries of origin to begin the work of reconstruction and renewal. I invite all here to consider how best to achieve a solution, and the Five States that will operate and control the technology, look forward to working with you." Within the hour, the Council President was on his way home.

Chapter 22

International Cooperation

Russian and Chinese troops together with control units from the Five States were dispatched to each country where the Islamic terrorists held sway and very quickly completed the task of disarming most of the enemy military machine.

It really was quite easy because of the simplicity of the technology to put together a workable repatriation program. Firstly the Chinese, with several million men and women under arms to draw on would, under the protection of the control system, advance into western Europe. They would then set up the grid system which was being operated and directed by the Five States, and create massive transit camps through which they held and then transported Islamic groups back to their countries or origin. It was the responsibility of the Russian troops, again, with the protection of the control system to literally corral the Islamists into the transit camps for onward return to their own country.

It was also Russia's task to disarm those Islamic terrorists who controlled certain African countries. The terrorists had made great inroads into Ethiopia, Libya, Sudan and Chad, but they had no answer to the power of the control system and were quickly and painlessly subdued. Of course, people deprived of their weaponry and who then become dependent on others for their food and drink tend to become very cooperative.

Once Islamic manpower started to arrive back in their own countries, construction teams were created to rebuild the infrastructure of those cities that had been destroyed. Rebuilding homes and commercial property was very much a long term project.

Other matters were attended to. British and American constitutional attorneys were retained to ensure that the countries previously occupied by the Caliphate would never again be controlled by families, dictators, despots or princes. Perhaps one of the most interesting things to emerge was that through it all, the Five States had come together and acted as one. They realized that collectively they were still the most powerful group on earth and a force for good.

Maybe the Five States should take another look at reconstruction and renewal insofar as it affects themselves. Maybe the United States could rise again but this time truly represent the people that it serves. Self interest is a thing of the past and perhaps the world is ready for a new type of leadership; one that promotes equality for all while leaving room for independent expression and reward.

Australia, due in part to its geographical location had been relatively immune to the Islamic problems suffered by Europe, Asia and Africa. That was about to change. Mrs. Jean McDonald, the popular Australian Prime Minister was listening to a presentation from her foreign secretary, Sam Wall.

"In short, Madam Prime Minister, Islam is gaining strength and support in Indonesia and with a Muslim population base of some 100 million people, this gives the terrorists a fertile base for recruitment. We are already dealing with increased levels of terrorist activity on the Australian mainland and if it spreads to Indonesia then the problem will be too big for us to handle. Madam Prime Minister, how do you wish to proceed?" ...

The End